The Strangest Stories From the Weirdest School

Michael Leviton

SCHOLASTIC INC.
New York Toronto London Auckland Sydney
Mexico City New Delhi Hong Kong Buenos Aires

**Illustrations
Nathan Jurevicius**

Copyright © 2004 by Scholastic Inc.
All rights reserved. Published by Scholastic Inc.
Printed in the U.S.A.

ISBN 0-439-70157-0

SCHOLASTIC, READ 180, and associated logos and designs are trademarks and/or registered trademarks of Scholastic Inc.

LEXILE is a registered trademark of MetaMetrics, Inc.

1 0   23   12 11

Contents

Introduction

A long time ago, people didn't have TV, books, or movies. So they made up their own stories. Some of these stories were really strange and weird.

The stories in this book are based on three old stories. They come from Poland, Nigeria, and Mexico. And all three stories are really weird.

The author of this book **updated** these tales. Now they happen in the present. They also happen in the same school. And it's not just any school. It's the weirdest school in the world!

updated made modern

In this story from Poland, some kids play a really good trick on a really mean girl.

1

The Meanest Girl

Louisa was a student at the weirdest school in the world. She was the richest girl in the whole school. She was also really mean.

The whole school was sick of her. "We must teach her a lesson!" everyone said. "Isabelle, help us!"

Isabelle was the smartest girl in school. "Okay," she said. "I'll play a trick on her."

Louisa wasn't nice at all. In fact, she was the meanest girl in school.

That afternoon, Isabelle walked up to Louisa. "Louisa," she said, "I have a problem. I want to take guitar lessons. But I don't have a guitar. Could I borrow yours?"

Louisa never missed a chance to brag. "I have 20 guitars!" she said. "Come over after school to get one."

Later that day, Isabelle visited Louisa's **mansion**. Louisa took her to the music room. She got out her oldest, ugliest guitar. Most of its strings were broken.

"Here you go, Isabelle," Louisa said, giggling. "Ha ha! Good luck!"

A week later, Isabelle went back to the mansion. She was carrying the guitar. And she had something else, too. She had a little **ukulele**! She had borrowed it from her friend Michael.

Louisa opened the door. Isabelle handed her the guitar. "Here's your guitar back," Isabelle said.

"You gave up so quickly!" Louisa said. "I guess that's smart. You would stink even if you practiced a lot! Ha ha!"

---

mansion a huge house
ukulele a musical instrument that looks like a small guitar

"Guess what!" Isabelle said to Louisa. "Your guitar had a baby!"

Isabelle just smiled. Then she said, "Wait! I almost forgot to tell you! Your guitar had a baby!" Then Isabelle pulled out the ukulele.

Louisa had never heard anything so crazy. She was about to laugh in Isabelle's face. But then she realized something. She wanted that ukulele. It was really cool.

"Oh yeah," Louisa said. "I remember now! That guitar did look sort of pregnant! Um, thanks." She grabbed the ukulele. Then she slammed the door.

A few days later, Isabelle asked Louisa for another favor.

"May I use your car?" Isabelle asked. "I want to visit a friend."

Of course, Louisa just had to brag. "I have six cars!" she said. She lent Isabelle the oldest, ugliest one.

Later that day, Isabelle returned the car. But she also brought along another surprise. She had her brother's motorcycle!

"Louisa, you're so lucky!" Isabelle said. "Your car gave birth to a motorcycle!"

Now Louisa *knew* Isabelle was crazy.

But she couldn't believe her good luck! She would look so cool on that motorcycle! "Thanks, Isabelle," she said. "Now get lost, loser!"

The next day, Isabelle had another favor to ask. "I have to go to a party, Louisa," she said. "May I borrow some of your jewelry?"

Louisa smiled. "Of course!" she said. Louisa was really happy about the ukulele and the motorcycle. So this time, she lent Isabelle her very best things. She filled a bag with diamond rings and pearl necklaces. Then she smiled **greedily**.

"These jewels look totally pregnant!" Louisa said. "I bet they'll have babies!"

Isabelle smiled. "Yeah, they do look kind of funny," she said.

greedily wanting more and more

Later that day, Isabelle sold all the jewelry. Now she was rich! She bought a new ukulele for Michael. She bought an awesome new motorcycle for her brother.

Then she split the rest of the money with the other kids from school. They threw a huge party!

The next day, Isabelle went to visit Louisa. Louisa was happy to see her. "Hello, my dear friend!" she shouted. "So, did my jewels have babies?"

"I'm sorry to have to tell you the bad news, Louisa," Isabelle said sadly. "But all your jewels died."

"What do you mean?" Louisa shouted.

"They died this morning," Isabelle said. "They must have been very sick."

"Jewels can't die!" Louisa screamed.

"What have you done with them?"

"I'm really sorry," Isabelle said. She patted Louisa.

"Give me back my jewels, you psycho!" Louisa yelled. But Isabelle only shook her head.

Louisa wanted those jewels back! And she knew just how to get them. She called up the *Judge Jane* TV show. She asked Judge Jane to hear her case.

"That judge will make Isabelle pay me back!" Louisa thought. "And I'll make Isabelle look stupid on TV!"

Judge Jane listened to Louisa's story. Louisa told the judge about the dead jewels. She told her about the pregnant guitar. She told her about the pregnant car, too.

"Louisa, you must listen to nonsense now, too," Judge Jane told her.

Then Louisa pointed at Isabelle. "She's crazy, your honor!" Louisa shouted. "Tell her to give me back my jewels!"

Judge Jane laughed. "Louisa, you listened to **nonsense** when it helped you. So you must also listen to nonsense when it hurts you. You happily took your guitar's baby. And you happily took your car's baby. So you should just have a funeral for your jewels! Case closed!"

Do you think Judge Jane's decision was fair? Why or why not?

nonsense stuff that makes no sense

Here's a story from Mexico.
Oscar is so lazy he'd rather be a bird!

2

The Laziest Boy

Oscar was the laziest boy at the weirdest school. His friends would ask him to play basketball. But he'd say, "No way! I'm not running all over that court! That's too much work!"

Girls would ask Oscar to go out. But he'd say, "No way! Kissing? Talking? Carrying heavy flowers? You can't trick me into doing all that work!"

"I don't want to do anything," Oscar would tell people.

His teachers would ask him to do homework. He'd say, "No, thanks, teacher. I'd rather just sit and do nothing."

Finally, Oscar's science teacher had an idea. "Oscar, you haven't done any work all year. But I'll forget about that if you do some now. Get an 'A' on this next project. Then I'll let you pass my class."

"A science project?" Oscar said. "No way! That sounds like work!"

The next day, Oscar met his new science partner. It was Sam. He was the hardest-working kid in school.

"Sam! This is perfect!" Oscar said. "You'll do all the work. And I won't do anything!"

Sam gave him a dirty look. "No way, Oscar!" he said.

Oscar sighed. "I guess I'm going to flunk," he thought.

Oscar walked home from school as slowly as he could. He felt sorry for himself the whole way. "I hate school! It's for the birds," he said to himself. "I wish I didn't have to go!"

Then he saw a **buzzard** in the sky. "Man," he thought. "What an easy life! Buzzards just fly around and eat. They don't go to school. They don't have science projects."

The buzzard flew down. It landed right next to him. Then it spoke! "Oscar," it said. "I hate being a buzzard. I'd rather go to school. Do you want to trade places?"

"And just fly around?" Oscar asked.

"It's not all flying," the buzzard told him. "You have to dive down to eat dead animals."

"So? I'll just **glide** down," Oscar said.

"Gliding looks easy," the buzzard said. "But it's hard. You can lose control!"

"Don't worry!" Oscar said. "I'll be a great buzzard!"

buzzard a big bird that feeds on dead animals
glide to move smoothly and easily

The buzzard put on Oscar's clothes. Oscar put on the bird's feathers.

So, the buzzard took off his feathers. And Oscar took off his clothes. Then the buzzard put on Oscar's clothes. And Oscar put on the feathers. They both looked pretty stupid. But Oscar felt happy.

"Okay," Oscar said. "I'll see you later, sucker!" He flapped his arms and took off into the sky. After a few minutes, he didn't feel so happy anymore. Flying wasn't fun. It was work!

"My arms are tired," Oscar complained. "This is worse than school. And I'm hungry, too."

Just then Oscar saw a dead cow on the ground. "Perfect!" he thought. He tried to glide down to it. But before long, he was out of control! He ran into a brick wall.

"I hate being a buzzard!" he screamed.

Meanwhile, the buzzard went to school. He got to class early. He started Oscar's science project. When Sam got there, he was surprised. "Wow, Oscar, you're working!"

"Sure I am," the buzzard said. "Work's not so bad."

Then Sam made a face. "Oscar!" he shouted. "Your breath stinks! Did you forget to brush your teeth? It smells like you ate a dead cat!"

"Oh . . . um . . . it's this science project. This stuff I'm using really stinks!" the buzzard said.

Soon, the buzzard and Sam became best friends. Their science project went very well, too.

One day, a girl named Sally asked the

buzzard on a date.

"I'd love to go out with you, Sally," the buzzard said. "You're so nice. And you're really hot, too!"

"Wow, Oscar," Sally said. "You're usually too lazy to go on dates. You must really like me!"

On the date, the buzzard brought candy and flowers. He made funny jokes. He seemed like the perfect boyfriend.

There was just one problem at dinner. After the buzzard finished his meal, he couldn't stop staring at Sally's food. He couldn't help it. He just wanted to swoop down and eat it.

"Could you please stop staring at my food," Sally said. "It's rude! You're like a **vulture!**"

vulture a bird that feeds on dead animals; it's like a buzzard

Sally started to kiss the buzzard. But then she got a terrible shock.

The buzzard pulled himself together. And after that, they had a great time. In fact, it was the best night of Sally's life.

At the end of the night, the buzzard brought Sally home. She moved in to kiss him. But then she got a horrible shock. Instead of lips, he had a beak!

"Wait a minute!" Sally said. "You're not Oscar! You're a buzzard wearing Oscar's clothes! No wonder you have bad breath!"

"Yes, it's true," the buzzard said. "I'm a buzzard, not a boy."

"Get away from me!" Sally screamed.

At school the next day, everyone made fun of the buzzard. People held their noses when he walked past.

The buzzard walked into science class. One kid said, "Good morning, bird brain!"

Another said, "Buzz off, buzzard!"

The buzzard felt terrible. He thought about quitting school.

Then Sam walked in. Sam was the buzzard's last hope. If Sam said something mean, too, he'd quit school for sure.

"Hi, Oscar," Sam said. "Everyone tells

The buzzard and Sam got an "A" on their project. Oscar kept crashing.

me you're a buzzard."

"It's true!" the buzzard said sadly.

"Well, I don't really care," Sam said. "I'd rather hang out with a hard-working buzzard than a lazy human!"

The buzzard felt better. He and Sam got to work. Soon, their project was done.

A week later, Sam and the buzzard got an "A" on their project. The buzzard was really proud. He stared out the window and dreamed about his future.

Then the buzzard saw Oscar in the sky. Oscar was trying to glide. But he kept crashing into trees!

"Poor Oscar," the buzzard thought. "The sky is no place for a lazy kid. But Oscar was right about one thing. School really is for the birds!"

This story is from Africa.
Rica's new boyfriend is perfect. Or is he?

3

The Snobbiest Girl

Rica was the hottest girl at the weirdest school. Everyone was in love with her.

But Rica's beauty didn't make her happy. And it didn't make her nice. In fact, Rica's beauty had made her totally snobby. "I hate ugly people!" she would say. "And this school is full of them! It's awful to be so beautiful in such an ugly place!"

It was spring. Prom was coming up.

Rica's beauty had made her totally snobby.

All the boys wanted to go with Rica. But she didn't think anyone was good enough for her.

When someone would ask Rica to the prom, she'd laugh. "Are you kidding?" she'd say. "You're too short! Your teeth aren't white enough. And your right ear is big!"

One of Rica's **admirers** was weirder than the rest. He wasn't a boy. He was just a big skull!

The skull knew he didn't have a chance. "Girls don't like skulls!" he complained. "Girls are into dumb stuff, like heads with faces and bodies. Who needs all that?" But to get Rica, *he* needed all that!

Then the skull had an idea. He went to see a friend. His friend was very handsome. "Can I borrow your face until prom?" the skull asked.

"No problem," the friend said.

The skull put on his friend's face. Then he went to see a friend who played soccer. "Can I borrow your legs?" the skull asked.

One by one, the skull visited all of his

---

admirers people who like someone

Rica had a strange secret admirer. A big skull had a crush on her!

friends. He borrowed their best parts. He put them on like a suit. Now the skull was the perfect guy!

The next day, the skull walked up to Rica. "Hey, baby, how are you doing?" he asked.

Rica was about to slap him. "Nobody

Rica fainted and fell right into the skull's perfect, borrowed arms.

calls me 'baby'!" she thought. But then she saw his perfect face.

Rica fainted. She fell right into the skull's perfect, borrowed arms.

"Are you okay?" the skull asked.

"No," she said. "I mean, yes." She couldn't speak.

"I'm in love with you," said the skull. "You're the most beautiful girl in *skull*— I mean *school*!" He laughed nervously. Rica smiled. The skull went on, "Will you go to prom with me?"

"We'll be the most beautiful couple there!" Rica said. "Looking good is my greatest skill!"

"Really? That's also my greatest *skull*— I mean *skill*," said the skull. The skull was really nervous. In fact, his borrowed body was sweating.

"Are you okay?" Rica asked.

"Yeah, I'm *skull*—I mean *cool*. I'm cool. I'm definitely not a skull. I'm just cool." The skull tried to smile.

Rica wasn't even listening. "My boyfriend is so hot!" Rica said. "Let's go outside and stare at each other!"

Rica and the skull held hands all day. Then, they held hands all week.

Finally, it was prom night. The skull picked up Rica at her house. Rica's dress was gold. She looked great. The skull wore a tuxedo. He looked perfect, too.

They drove to the dance. They walked onto the dance floor. Everyone gasped. No one had ever seen such a good-looking couple.

As usual, Rica was really snobby. "You don't have to stare!" she told the other kids. "We know how good we look!"

A girl said, "So what? Looking good isn't everything."

Rica made a face. "It's not my fault you're ugly!" she said.

The band played a slow song. Rica and the skull danced closely. Rica shut her eyes. It was the best moment of her life.

Just then, the skull saw a friend crawling toward him. The friend said, "Hey skull, the whole gang is playing basketball. I need my legs back!"

"I can't give them back now!" the skull whispered. "I'm dancing with the girl of my dreams!"

But his friend wouldn't wait. "Come on, skull! They're *my* legs! You've had them for a week!"

"Oh, okay," the skull said. "Here you go." He pulled off the legs.

Everyone pointed and screamed. But Rica's eyes were still closed. She was so happy she didn't even notice the screams!

The skull tried to stay cool. But then another friend walked in. "Hey skull!" he shouted. "The guys are playing basketball! I need my arms!"

The skull put a finger to his lips. "Ssshh!" he said. He didn't want to bother Rica.

Quietly, he handed back one of his arms. His friend grabbed the other one. Rica still didn't notice!

One by one, the skull's other friends walked in. And one by one, they asked for their body parts. After a while, everyone stopped screaming and started laughing!

Finally, Rica noticed something. "You feel light as a feather!" she said. She opened her eyes. She saw that she was holding a skull! She looked around the room. All the kids were pointing and laughing.

Rica was so happy, she didn't notice she was dancing with a skull!

Rica screamed. She threw the skull on the ground.

"Look, I'm sorry I'm just a skull," he said. "But I still love you!"

Then a guy with a microphone walked onto the dance floor and said, "It's time to crown our prom king and queen. And the winners are Rica and her date!"

The kids grabbed Rica and the skull. They put crowns on the couple's heads. Then they sat them on a giant throne.

"They're perfect for each other!" one boy said.

"Yeah, her head's just as empty as the skull's!" one girl joked.

Then everyone became quiet. It was time for the prom queen's speech.

Rica took the mike and said, "You think

I'm embarrassed. But I'm not!" She smiled beautifully and said, "There's nothing embarrassing about going to prom with the perfect boy! If I had gone to prom with one of you ugly losers, *that* would have been embarrassing!"

The skull smiled. He had a hopeful look in his hollow eyes. He turned to Rica and said, "Really? You mean it?"

"Yeah," Rica said.

"Great," the skull said. "So, you'll still be my girlfriend?"

Do you think Rica will be any different after the prom?

Glossary

admirers *(noun)* people who like someone

buzzard *(noun)* a big bird that feeds on dead animals

glide *(verb)* to move smoothly and easily

greedily *(adverb)* wanting more and more

mansion *(noun)* a huge house

nonsense *(noun)* stuff that makes no sense

ukulele *(noun)* a musical instrument that looks like a small guitar

updated *(verb)* made modern

vulture *(noun)* a bird that feeds on dead animals; it's like a buzzard